Moonlight

By Helen V. Griffith

Illustrations by Laura Dronzek

Greenwillow Books
An Imprint of HarperCollinsPublishers

Acrylic paints were used to prepare the full-color art.

The text type is 32-point Adobe Jenson.

Library of Congress Cataloging-in-Publication Data

Griffith, Helen V.

Moonlight / by Helen V. Griffith ; illustrations by Laura Dronzek.

p. cm.

"Greenwillow Books."

Summary: One cloudy night, after Rabbit goes into his burrow

to sleep, the moon comes out, covering the countryside like butter

and awakening Rabbit to come out and dance.

ISBN 978-0-06-203285-0 (trade bdg.) — ISBN 978-0-06-203286-7 (lib. bdg.)

[1. Stories in rhyme. 2. Moon—Fiction. 3. Rabbits—Fiction.]

I. Dronzek, Laura, ill. II. Title.

PZ8.3.G876Moo 2012   [E]—dc22   2011002149

12 13 14 15 16 SCP 10 9 8 7 6 5 4 3 2 1

First Edition

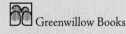 Greenwillow Books

For Jack—H.V.G.

For Susan—L.D.

Rabbit hides in shadow
under cloudy skies
waiting for the moonlight
blinking sleepy eyes

hops into his burrow
just a little soon

doesn't see the clouds blow by
setting free the moon.

Moonlight slides like butter

skims through outer space
skids past stars and comets

leaves a butter trace

skips along the mountainside

butters every tree

sucks at twigs and branches
like a butter bee

skitters down the tree trunks

slips into the streams

seeps inside the burrow

butters Rabbit's dreams

spatters him with moondrops
shakes him out of bed—

Rabbit dances in the field
butter on his head!